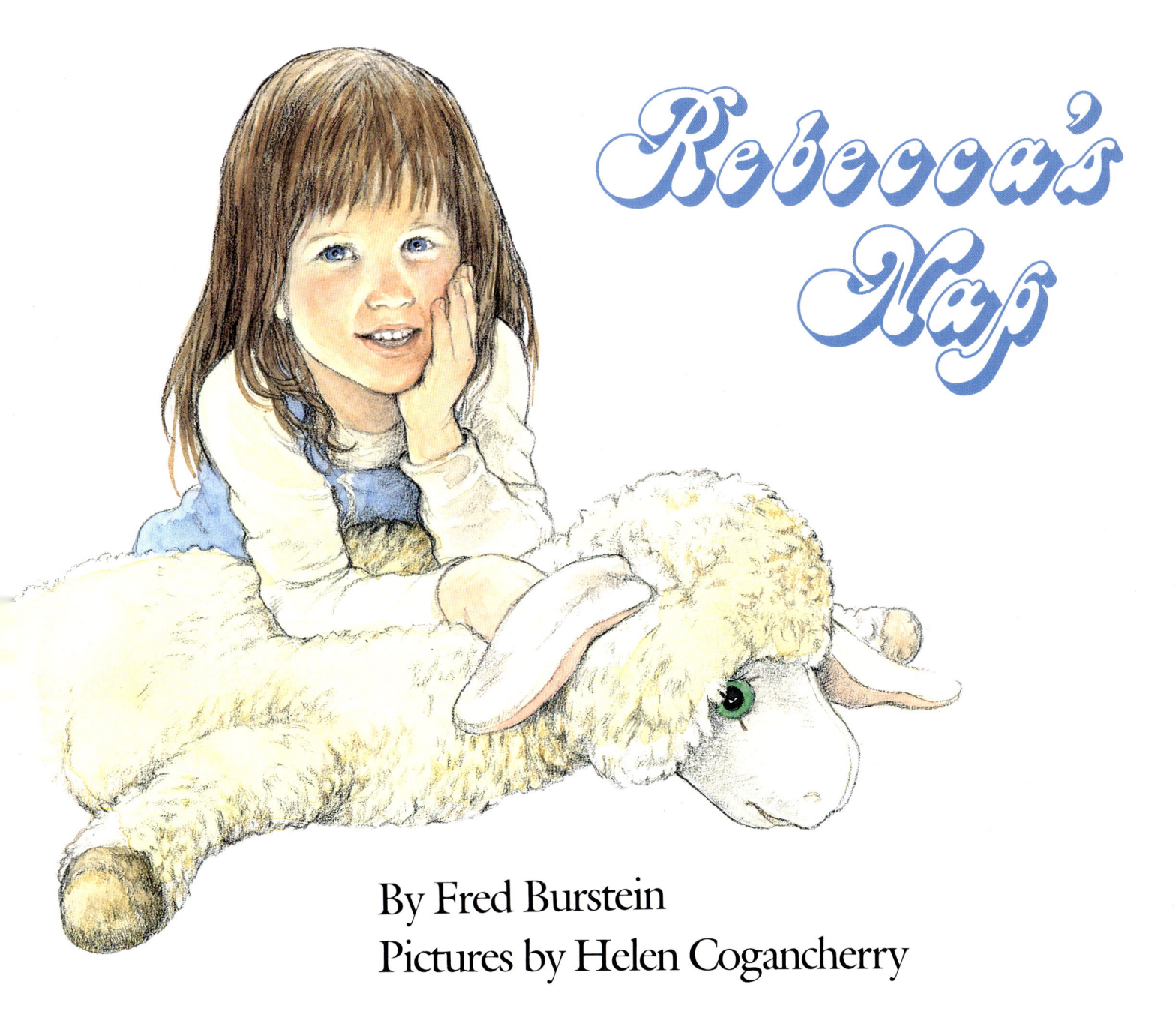

# Rebecca's Nap

By Fred Burstein
Pictures by Helen Cogancherry

BRADBURY PRESS    NEW YORK

Thank you, Joe Hardy, Richard Jackson,
and Barbara Lalicki, for your help and care
with *Rebecca's Nap*. —F. B.

Text copyright © 1988 by Fred Burstein
Illustrations copyright © 1988 by Helen Cogancherry

All rights reserved. No part of this book may be reproduced or
transmitted in any form or by any means, electronic or mechanical,
including photocopying, recording, or by any information storage
and retrieval system, without permission in writing from the Publisher.

Bradbury Press
An Affiliate of Macmillan, Inc.
866 Third Avenue, New York, N.Y. 10022
Collier Macmillan Canada, Inc.
Printed and bound in Japan
10 9 8 7 6 5 4 3 2 1

The text of this book is set in 24 pt. ITC Galliard.
The illustrations are watercolor and colored pencil.

LIBRARY OF CONGRESS CATALOGING-IN-PUBLICATION DATA

Burstein, Fred.
 Rebecca's nap/story by Fred Burstein; illustrations by
Helen Cogancherry.
   p.  cm.
  Summary: Rebecca, Daddy, and Mommy have different ideas about nap time.
  ISBN 0-02-715620-6
  [1. Sleep—Fiction.  2. Bedtime—Fiction.]  I. Cogancherry,
Helen, ill.  II. Title.
PZ7.B945534Re 1988
[E]—dc 19    88-1041    CIP    AC

For Anna and Rebecca and Fran
—F. B.

To my daughter, Lynne, who loves the woods
—H.C.

"Rebecca," Daddy said.

"No, Daddy. I won't take a nap," Rebecca said.

But soon she was fast asleep.

"I'll take her up to bed," Mommy said.
"Then I'll take a nap, too."

"Sleep tight, my love."

"Sweet dreams," Daddy said.
"I'll be outside."

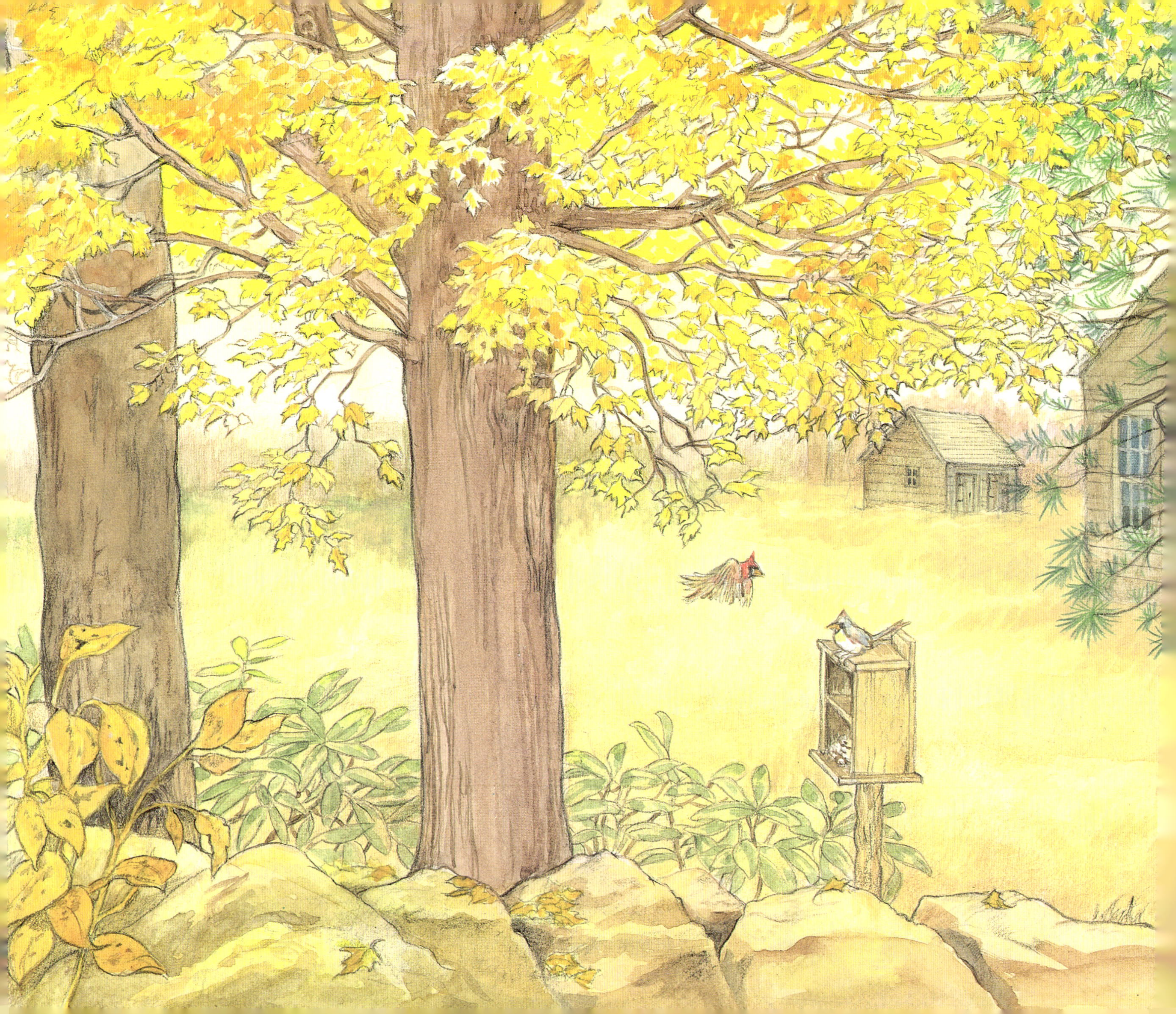

"Oh, Daddy.
Oh, Daddy.
Oh, Daddy."

"Shh. Here I am."

"I woke up, Daddy."

"Mommy's asleep. Let's go outside and look around," Daddy said. "Just you and me."

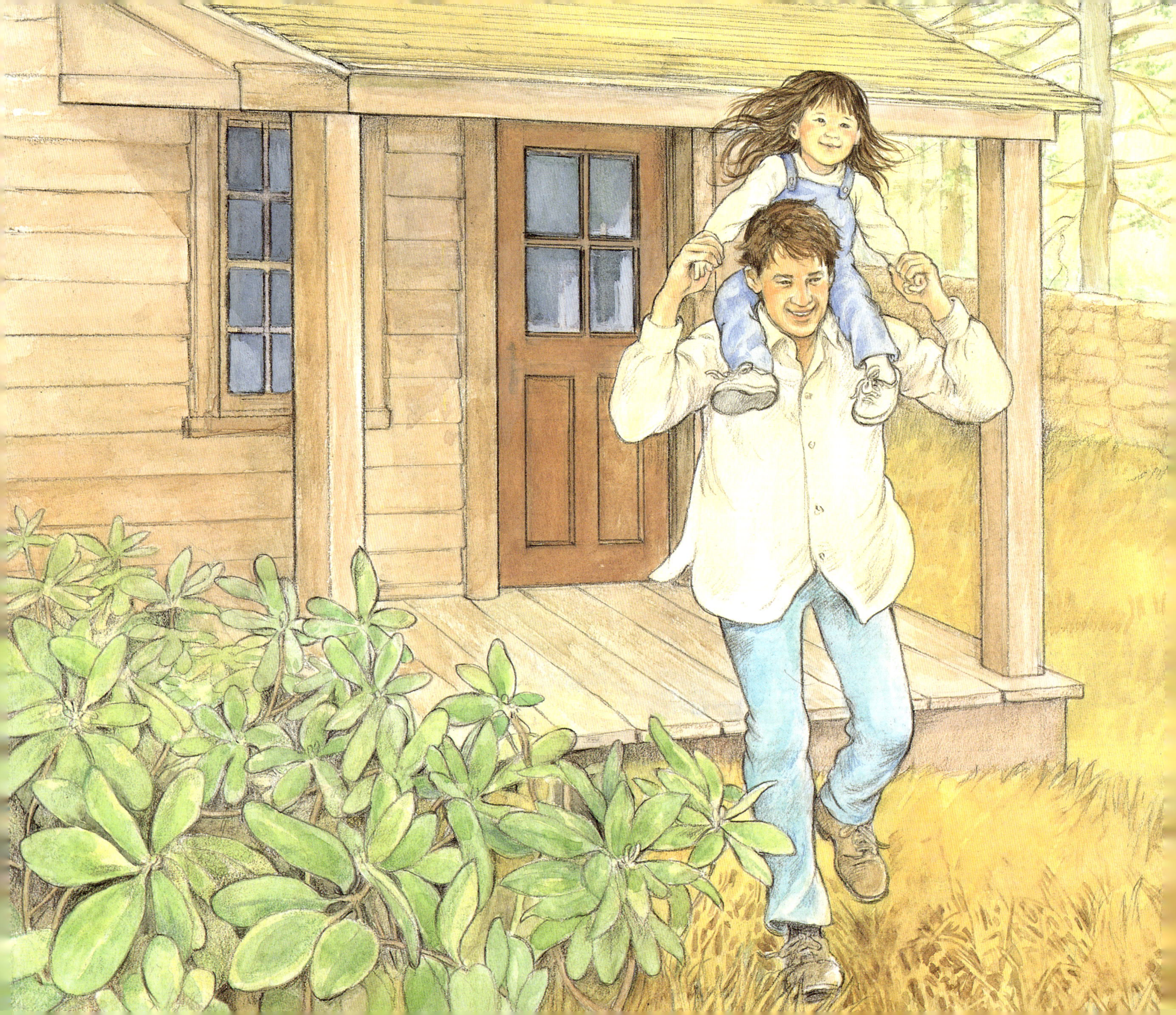

"You're a good boy, Daddy."

"Can I look in the fox den?" Rebecca asked.

"No, baby. If she's there, she might nip your nose."

"She won't, Daddy. She won't nip my nose. Let. Me. Go."

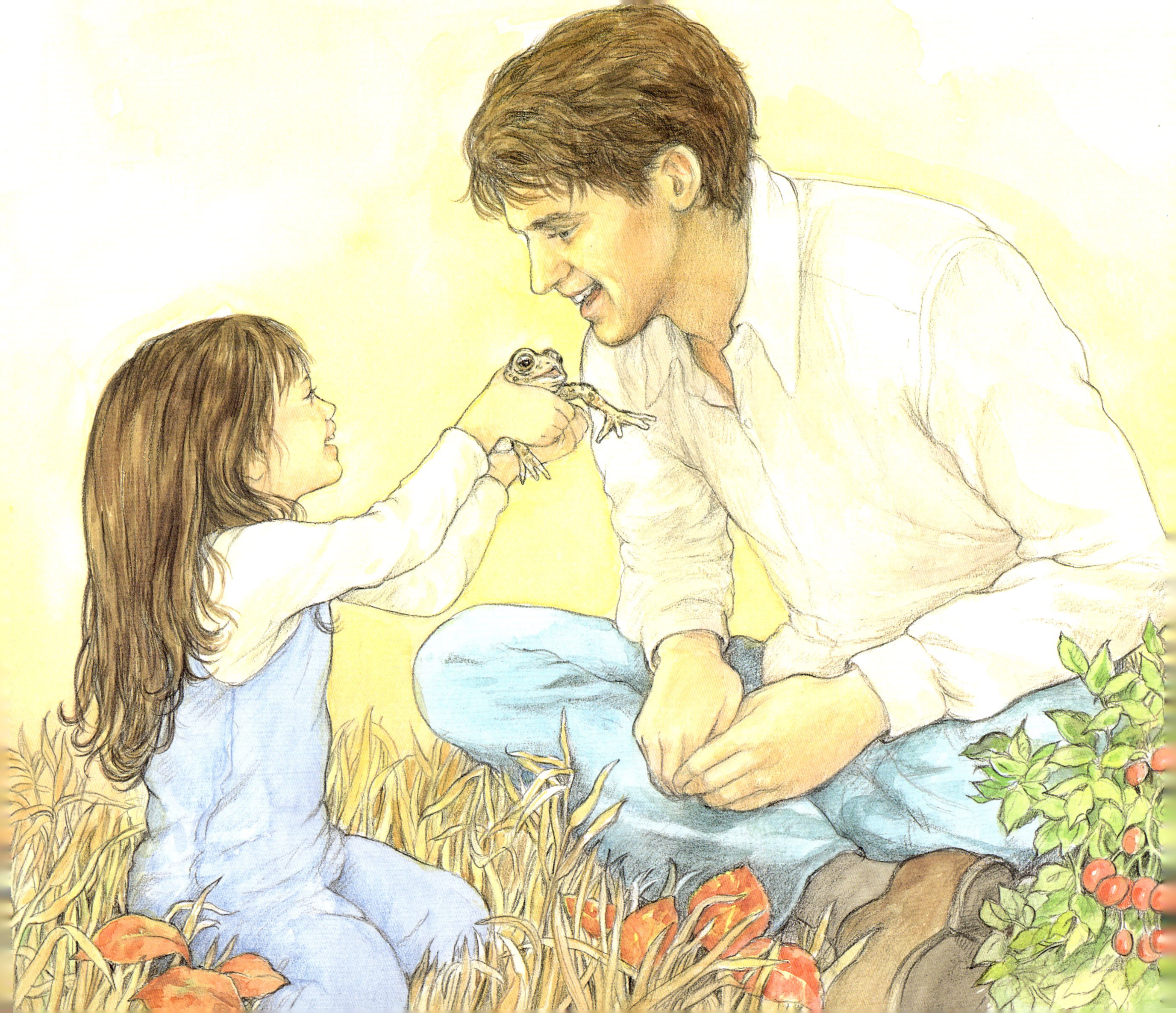

"Look, Daddy. A big fat toad. I'll put him in the garden and he can eat bugs all day."

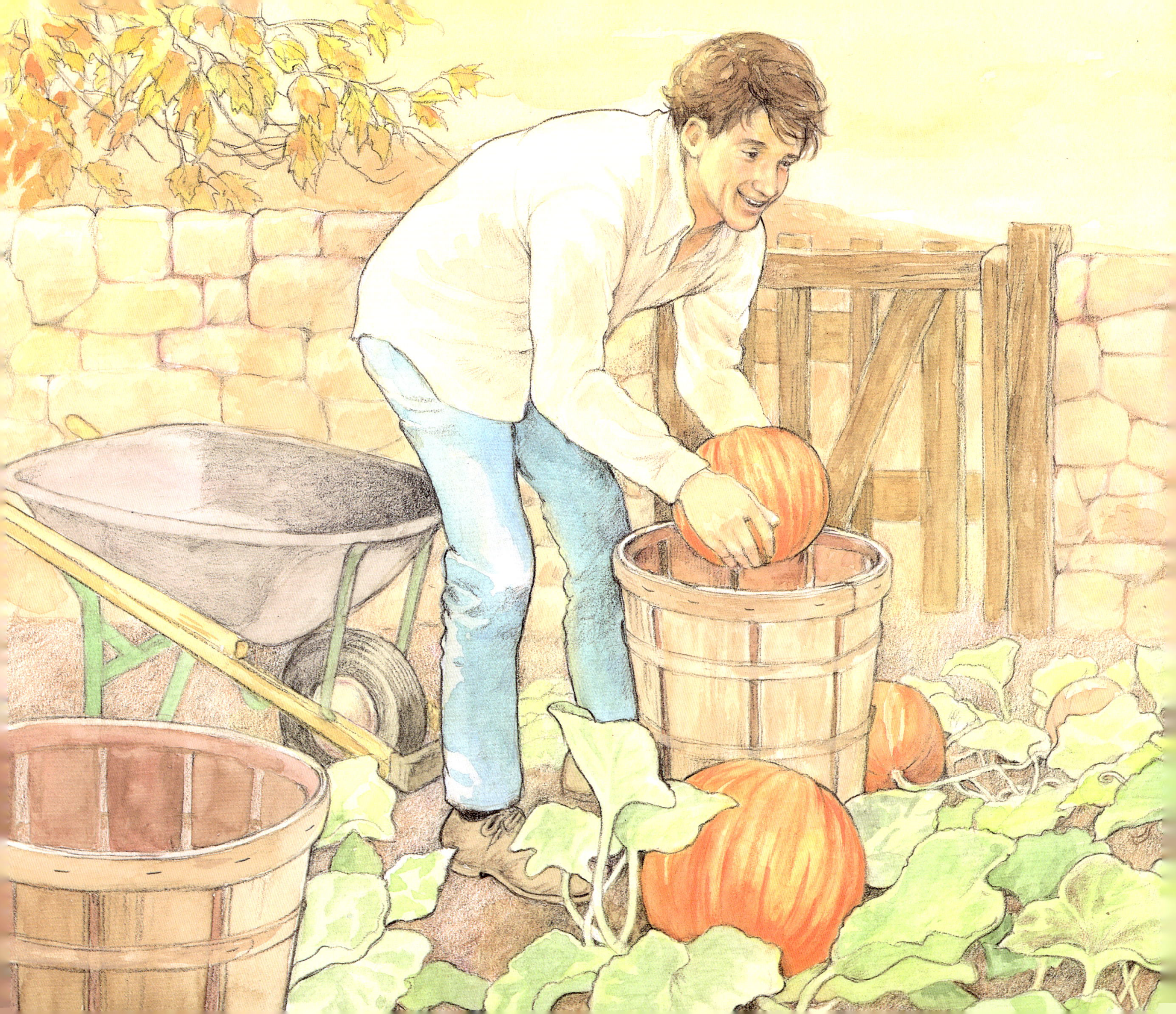

"Giddy-up, pumpkin. Come on. Faster. Faster."

"I gave Cricket an apple, Daddy. All by myself."

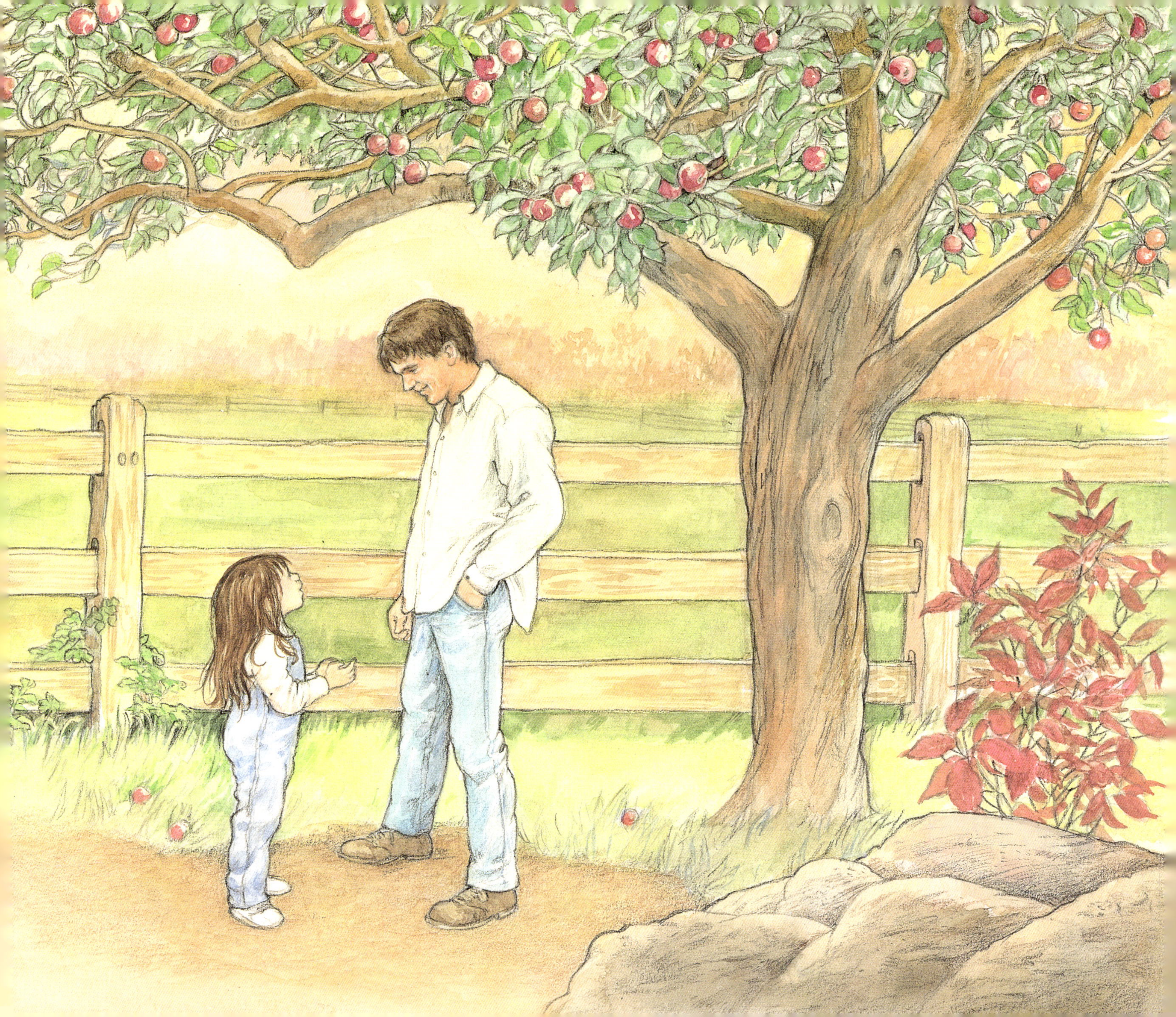

"It's getting cold.
   Come home and we'll build a fire."

"I won't go home."

"Rebecca, look. There she is.
There's the fox on our own stone wall."

"I'm sleeping, Daddy."

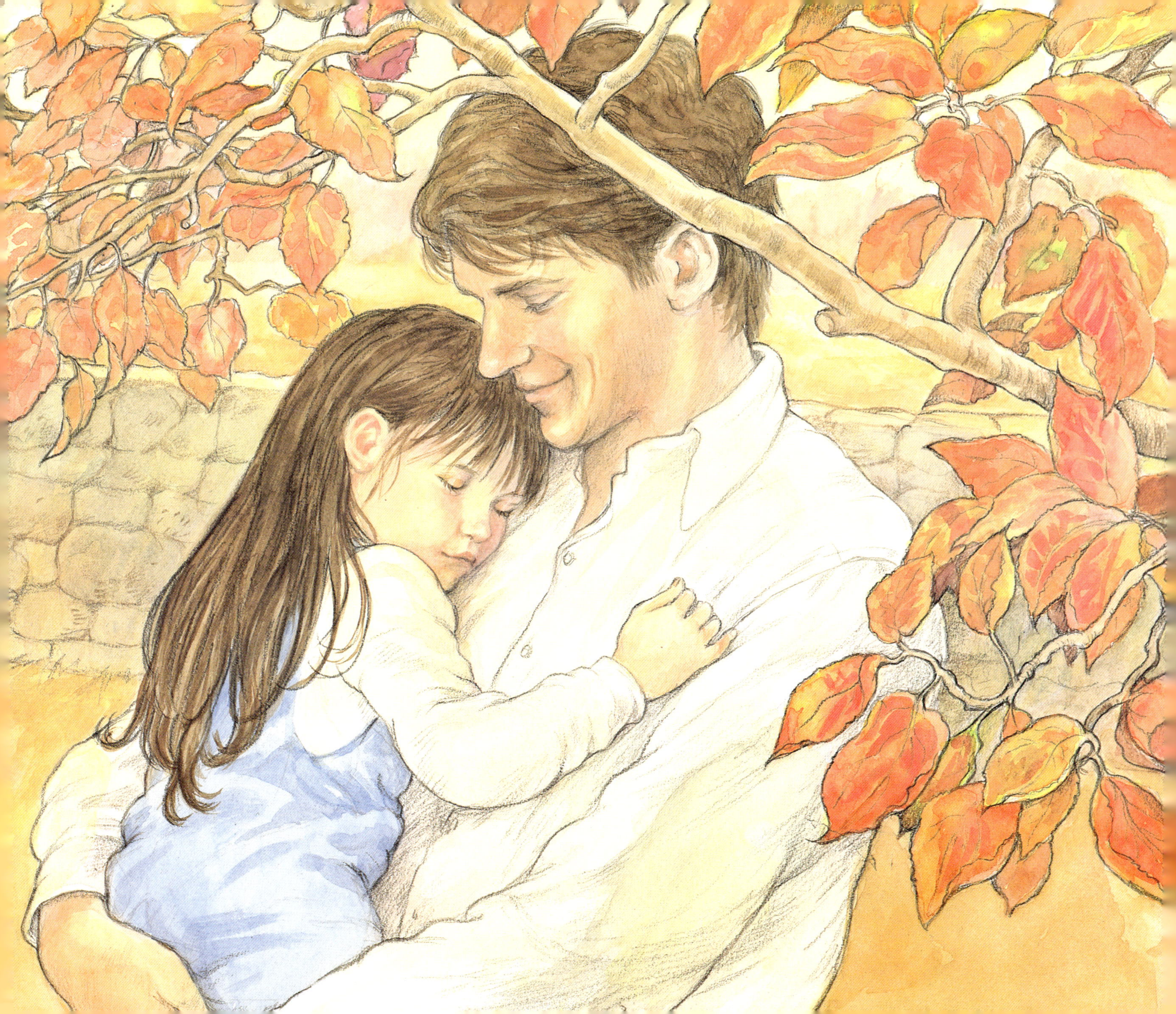

"Sweet dreams, my love."

"What a sleepyhead," Mommy whispered.

"I think there's a fox outside, Mommy."

"Shh. Daddy's asleep. You and I can go look."

"Just a minute, Mommy," Rebecca whispered. "I have to kiss Daddy good-bye."